The Birthday Card

Shirley Isherwood

Illustrated by Rowan Clifford

To Parents

How to read this book together

- You, as the Storyteller, read the words at the bottom of each page.

- After you have read your part, ask your child to join in with the words in the speech bubbles, and point to the words as they are read.

Remember young children love repetition — it builds their confidence in reading. Always praise good guesses, and if your child is stuck just give the word yourself. This is far more helpful than sounding out individual letters.

The Riddlers of Riddleton End

Talk about the characters your child may have met in **The Riddlers** TV series. There's wise Mossop and his young friend Tiddler, who live at the bottom of the well in Marjorie Daw's garden, and have lots of adventures with Postie the hedgehog and Filbert the squirrel. The books also introduce some new characters — Harvest Mouse, Frog, The Dawn Fairy and a family of mischievous voles.

The Riddlers is a ♥ Yorkshire Television Production.

It was Marjorie's birthday and Tiddler and Mossop made her a birthday card.

Tiddler set off down the garden to
put the card through Marjorie's
letter box. Suddenly, a gust of wind
blew the card out of her hand.

Tiddler couldn't see where the card
had gone.
"I've lost the birthday card!"
she cried.

7

Just then, Postie came through the gap in the hedge. His spikes were full of letters.

"I've lost Marjorie's birthday card," said Tiddler.

"Don't worry," said Postie. "I'll help you find it."

9

The card had blown onto a lily pad
on the pond. Frog was sitting on the
lily pad looking at it.
"What's that?" asked Frog.

10

"It's Marjorie's birthday card," said Tiddler. So Frog jumped from the lily pad and gave the card back to her.

11

"The card's wet," said Tiddler.
"Don't worry," said Postie. "You can
put it in the sun to dry."

12

So Tiddler and Postie sat and
waited for the card to dry.

13

Then Tiddler set off down the path.
On the way, she met Harvest Mouse.

"What's that?" asked Harvest Mouse.
"It's Marjorie's birthday card,"
said Tiddler.

15

So Tiddler took the card and
showed it to her. Harvest Mouse
held it in her tiny paws.

16

When she gave it back there were paw prints on it.

"The card's full of smudges,"
said Tiddler.
"Don't worry," said Postie. "You can
rub them away."

18

So Postie gave Tiddler the rubber
that he carried on his spikes and
she rubbed the smudges away.

Tiddler set off down the path once
more. On the way, she met the
family of voles coming out of the

20

long grass. They snatched the
birthday card and ran away with it.

So Tiddler went to find Postie.
"The voles have taken Marjorie's birthday card!" she said.
"Don't worry," said Postie. "I'll help you find them."

22

So Tiddler and Postie went to look
for the voles.

They found the voles with their
mother, and everyone was looking
at the card.

24

"It's a nice birthday card," they said, and then gave it back to Tiddler. But the card was torn.

"The card's torn," said Tiddler. "Don't worry," said Postie. "You can mend it with sticky tape."

26

So Postie gave Tiddler some sticky
tape to mend the tear. Then,
Tiddler set off again to Marjorie's
house with the card.

Everyone went with her — Mossop,
Postie, Frog, Harvest Mouse and the
family of voles.

28

They all stood together on
Marjorie's doorstep and sang,
"Happy Birthday."